MW01079466

BLUEBONNET
at Johnson
Space Center

Mary Brooke Casad

BLUEBONNET
at Johnson Space Center

Illustrated by
Benjamin Vincent

PELICAN PUBLISHING COMPANY

GRETNA 1993

For future space travelers McCrae, Carter, Christopher, Matthew, Andrew, and Erin Brooke

The word "Pelican" and the depiction of a pelican are trademarks of Pelican Publishing Company, Inc., and are registered in the U.S. Patent and Trademark Office.

Library of Congress Cataloging-in-Publication Data
Casad, Mary Brooke.
    Bluebonnet at Johnson Space Center/Mary Brooke Casad; illustrated by Benjamin Vincent.
        p.   cm.
    Summary: Bluebonnet the armadillo visits the Lyndon B. Johnson Space Center in Houston and takes a ride on the space shuttle.
    ISBN 0-88289-963-5
    [1. Armadillos—Fiction. 2. Space shuttles—Fiction. 3. Astronautics—Fiction. 4. Lyndon B. Johnson Space Center—Fiction.] I. Vincent, Benjamin, ill. II. Title.
PZ7.C265Bm   1993
[E]—dc20   92-37416
                                                    CIP
                                                    AC

Manufactured in Hong Kong

Published by Pelican Publishing Company, Inc.
1101 Monroe Street, Gretna, Louisiana 70053

BLUEBONNET AT JOHNSON SPACE CENTER

Bluebonnet was an armadillo who loved to see the sights of Texas. Because she wore a bright blue sunbonnet, she was often seen by Texans as she roamed around the hills and the prairies, searching for new adventures and friends.

Now one day, Bluebonnet set out on a journey to Houston to visit her sister Normadillo. It had been a long time since they were little dillos growing up with their sisters Irmadillo and Arvilladillo in the Texas Hill Country. The four armadillo sisters were now grown. Each one lived in a different part of Texas.

When Bluebonnet arrived in Houston, she first went to Normadillo's burrow.

"Normadillo!" she called, peeking into the burrow.

"Bluebonnet? Is that you?" Up popped Normadillo's head. "So you finally made it to Houston!"

"Yes!" said Bluebonnet, hugging her sister. "I am a traveling Texas armadillo, and I've come to do some sight-seeing in Houston. What can I see while I'm here?"

Suddenly, Normadillo's eyes grew big. She gasped with excitement:

"Do you remember how we used to look up at the stars on summer nights in the Hill Country? Remember how you wished you could travel in outer space?"

Bluebonnet smiled at her sister. "Yes, I do," she said. "I would pretend that I was an astrodillo, traveling in a spaceship to visit other planets." She looked up at the sky and tried to imagine herself dressed in a space suit and helmet. "But what does that have to do with my trip to Houston?" she asked.

"There's a place here that I want you to see," said Normadillo. "The Lyndon B. Johnson Space Center. NASA!"

"NASA?" Bluebonnet asked. "What does that mean?"

"National Aeronautics and Space Administration," said Normadillo. "At the Johnson Space Center, we'll be able to learn about rockets and astronauts and outer space!"

"My, my," said Bluebonnet. "That *is* exciting! Do you know the way to Johnson Space Center? Have you visited there before? Can we go now?"

Normadillo laughed. "Calm down, you silly dilly!" she said. "*Yes* — to all three of your questions."

The two armadillo sisters left Normadillo's burrow and began walking. Soon they were entering the gates of the Johnson Space Center. They ambled up to the Space Center Houston building.

"Wow!" exclaimed Bluebonnet. "This is incredible." As the two armadillos sneaked into the circular center, they looked above and around them. They could see replicas of a space shuttle and other spacecraft. Many people walked about, looking at the exhibits, but they didn't see the little armadillos who darted across the floor.

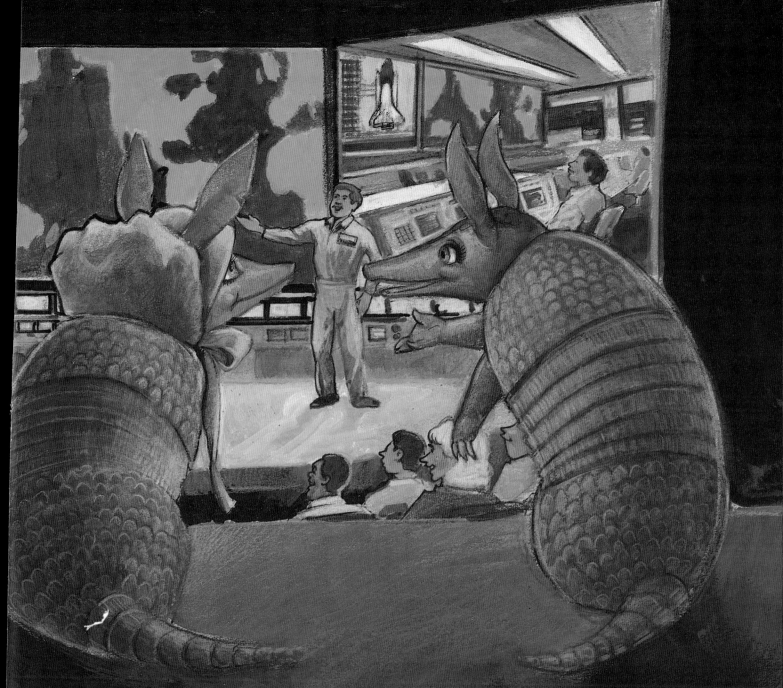

"Let's start with the Mission Status Center," said Normadillo. "The news broadcast will show us what space missions are in progress today."

Bluebonnet and Normadillo watched the live camera reports and listened to the mission briefing officer.

"As you can see on our cameras, the Space Shuttle is in place at the Kennedy Space Center launch pad," the officer said. At that moment a picture of the upright thirty-story-high space shuttle flashed on the screen. Attached to the shuttle was a large orange fuel tank and two white rockets that would provide the needed lift-off into space. "The next shuttle mission will begin in a few days," said the officer.

"Oh, Normadillo, wouldn't it be fun to watch it blast off?" Bluebonnet asked her sister.

Normadillo nodded in agreement. "The space shuttle can fly like a jet," she said. "It rides on the rockets to get into orbit, but it comes back to Earth and lands on its own."

"I keep trying to imagine what it feels like in outer space," said Bluebonnet.

"Well, Bluebonnet, the next best thing to being in space is 'The Feel of Space,'" said Normadillo. She guided Bluebonnet to the next area, being careful to stay out of the other visitors' sight.

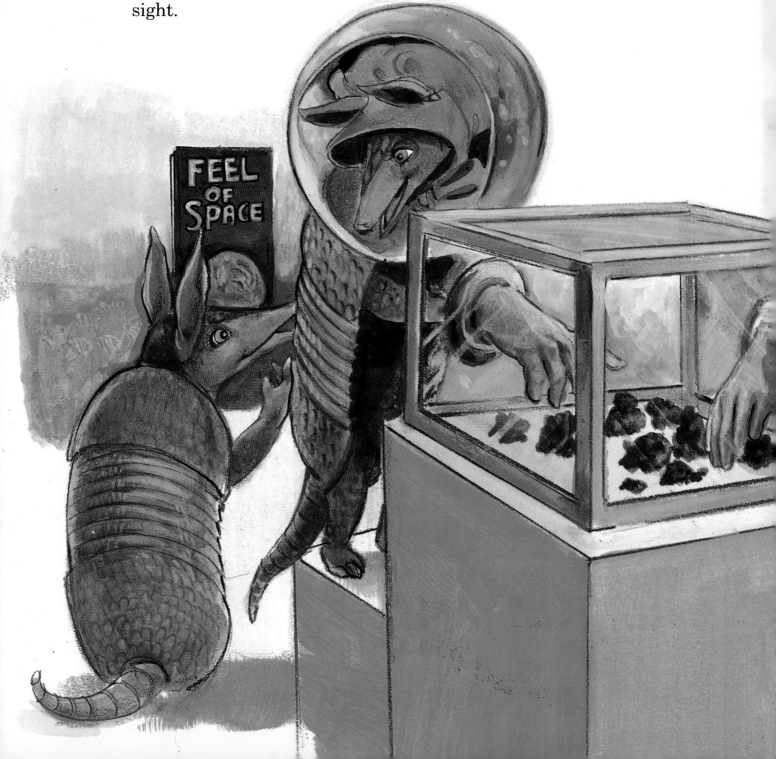

Normadillo helped her sister put on a space helmet. Then, she slipped her tiny paw into a pressurized space glove.

"Oh, my goodness," Bluebonnet gasped. "So this is what an astronaut's space suit feels like."

"If you think that's neat, how would you like to see the inside of a space shuttle?" asked Normadillo.

Bluebonnet removed the glove and helmet and followed her sister. They climbed up the steep stairs and crept through the small opening in the side of the shuttle. There was no one inside.

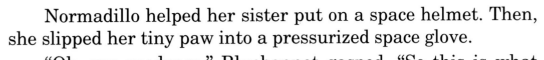

"Look, Bluebonnet," said Normadillo. "Here's where the astronauts are strapped in for the launch. When they orbit the earth, they can float around the cabin."

Bluebonnet looked at the galley. "This is the kitchen," she said. She looked at the food compartments and oven. There were packages of dried foods. "It must be hard to eat floating food!"

Normadillo laughed. "And look how they sleep," she said. "These sleeping bags are attached to the wall."

Bluebonnet noticed that the walls of the shuttle had small storage compartments. "Each astronaut has a place to store his or her belongings," Normadillo told her. "This is also where they store the items used in scientific experiments."

Bluebonnet looked at the control panel. She pretended to be the pilot. "This is Bluebonnet to Mission Control. Come in!" she said. "Mission Control? Do you read me?"

"I read you loud and clear!" said Normadillo. "Come on. We've got lots more to see."

Reluctantly, Bluebonnet followed her sister out of the space shuttle. They walked into the Space Center theater behind a crowd of tourists.

"See all the different space suits?" said Normadillo, pointing to the display. "The suits are heavy on Earth, but in space, they are weightless."

"They look pretty heavy to me," said Bluebonnet. She looked at the portraits on the wall of every American astronaut who had traveled in space. For just a second, Bluebonnet let herself imagine that her picture was on the wall, too.

Normadillo came up behind her. "Are you pretending that your picture is hanging in the astronaut gallery?" she asked, giving her sister a wink.

Bluebonnet blushed and blinked and stammered, "Well . . . sort of . . ."

Normadillo laughed. "You silly dilly! Come on, let's go into the theater."

Strolling into the now darkened theater, they found their seats and looked up in awe at the huge screen. The movie, *To Be an Astronaut,* told about the training that astronauts receive at the Johnson Space Center.

"It certainly takes a lot of hard work, doesn't it?" Normadillo whispered to her sister.

"Yes," Bluebonnet whispered back, nodding her head. "Astronauts have to learn a lot in school, especially in math and science. Then, they have to prepare for the physical demands of space travel."

The two armadillos watched in fascination as the movie described the special airplanes and machines that produced the "zero gravity" effect for the astronauts to train in.

"Hmmm," thought Bluebonnet to herself. "To be an astrodillo!"

Normadillo thumped her sister with her tail, interrupting Bluebonnet's daydream. "Do you want to see a real astronaut?"

Bluebonnet nodded, blinking her eyes as the lights came on in the dark theater. The two sisters followed the crowd back out of the theater to the Space Center Plaza.

"Every afternoon, astronauts, scientists, and engineers tell about the current space projects they are working on," said Normadillo.

A group of people had already gathered around a small platform where several men and women stood. Bluebonnet and Normadillo found a hidden spot where they could see the program, too.

"What are they saying?" Bluebonnet asked.

"These are the astronauts who will be flying on the next space shuttle mission," said Normadillo. "The announcer says that they will be conducting experiments to gather information for the future mission to Mars."

"Aren't they lucky?" Bluebonnet sighed. "I wish I could go with them."

"Our tour is not over yet, Bluebonnet," said Normadillo, nudging her sister towards the door. "We're going to visit some other buildings. Mission Control Center is located in Building 30."

The armadillo sisters walked outside as the talk ended and the people moved away. Bluebonnet noticed the flower beds next to the sidewalks. "Before we go on, let's find some insects to eat," she said.

"Good idea!" said Normadillo. "I am getting hungry."

The two armadillos began to dig beneath the bushes for their food. They overheard a group of scientists talking as they walked by.

"If we could perform this experiment on the next space shuttle flight, we could learn some valuable information that would help us prepare for the mission to Mars," said a voice.

"Yes, but we will need an armadillo to help us," said another voice. "Where can we get one?"

"Why, this is Texas!" said yet another voice. "There are lots of armadillos in Texas."

"Well," said the first voice, "we just need one. Studying the armadillo shell and the way the plates permit the armadillo to curl up in a ball should provide us with important data in designing new space suits."

"Normadillo!" Bluebonnet exclaimed. She stopped digging and listened carefully. "Did you hear that? They need an armadillo to go on the space shuttle! I want to go!"

"Now, Bluebonnet," Normadillo cautioned her sister, "I don't think that's a wise idea. You don't know what this is all about."

"But, Normadillo, it's a chance to make my dream of becoming an astrodillo come true," Bluebonnet pleaded.

"Bluebonnet, that was a lot of fun to pretend when we were little dillos," Normadillo said in a no-nonsense manner. "But we're grown up now and . . ."

"But that doesn't mean that my dreams have changed," Bluebonnet said. "What it means is that I have to try even harder to make those dreams come true." Bluebonnet took a deep breath. "I'm going to volunteer," she told her sister firmly.

"You are not!" said Normadillo, grabbing at her sister's tail.

"I am, too!" said Bluebonnet, and she stepped out from behind the bushes and in front of the scientists.

"Why . . . it's an armadillo!" they exclaimed.

"I told you there are lots of armadillos in Texas," said one of the scientists. He bent down and picked up Bluebonnet. "But I've never seen one wearing a sunbonnet before."

"A blue sunbonnet," said another voice. "We'll call her Bluebonnet, after the state flower of Texas."

Bluebonnet smiled. She could hear Normadillo squealing an armadillo message to her to jump down and run away.

"It's okay, Normadillo," she squealed back. "They even know my name!"

The scientists talked excitedly as they carried Bluebonnet to another building. "At the Weightless Environment Training Facility, we'll be able to see how Bluebonnet will perform on a space walk," one of the scientists said.

Bluebonnet fidgeted around. She was excited about being an astrodillo, but she wasn't sure what to expect.

When they entered the building, Bluebonnet saw a large swimming pool.

"The pool is twenty-five feet deep. It helps us practice for the weightless conditions of space," said the man who was carrying her. He put her down beside the pool.

"Oh, dear!" Bluebonnet thought to herself as she peered into the pool. "It is very deep!"

Then, she smiled and thought to herself, "I'll go swimming the armadillo way." And with that, she took a deep breath and plunged into the pool. Down, down she dropped. When she reached the bottom, she jumped up and curled into a ball.

"Whee!" she cried as she spun around in circles in the water. Up, up she came until she reached the top.

The scientists applauded and cheered. "Looks like you're a natural for space travel," her new friends praised her.

Bluebonnet was put on an airplane and flown with some of her scientist friends to Kennedy Space Center in Cape Canaveral, Florida. Early on the day of the launch, Bluebonnet was placed in the astronaut van. The astronauts she had seen from a distance at the Johnson Space Center greeted her.

"Hello, Bluebonnet," they said. "We're glad you're with us."

Bluebonnet smiled at her new astronaut friends. She knew that they shared her dreams of traveling through space. They had trained and prepared for this moment for many long years.

The van headed for the launch pad. When they arrived, Bluebonnet craned her neck to look up at the shuttle, which towered 195 feet above the ground. Off in the distance, she could see the Atlantic Ocean.

An elevator in the launch tower took Bluebonnet and the astronauts to a level near the nose of the space shuttle. They walked across an access arm and into a small room, next to the space shuttle's hatch, where technicians were waiting to help.

"Hello, Bluebonnet," said one of the technicians. "We're ready to climb aboard the shuttle."

Bluebonnet and the technician went through the small hatch. They were on the space shuttle! Carefully, the technician strapped special belts across Bluebonnet's shelled back.

"Now, Bluebonnet," said the technician, "here's a special 'Snoopy cap' made just for you." He placed a helmet on her head. "The speakers in the earflaps let you hear the commands from Mission Control. There's also a microphone, and oxygen supply."

"One hour until lift-off," he said. Bluebonnet watched as the other technicians strapped the astronauts into their special seats. They were wearing their launch helmets and lying on their backs, facing the nose of the shuttle. The technicians left and closed the hatch behind them.

Through the shuttle windows Bluebonnet could see the launch tower and the clear, blue sky. "I wish Normadillo could see me now," she sighed wistfully to herself.

The countdown began.

"Ten, nine, eight, seven, six, five, four, three, two, one . . . ," a voice counted over the speakers. Bluebonnet heard a loud roar and felt the rumbling beneath her as the booster rockets ignited and the shuttle began to move upwards.

"Oh, dear," gasped Bluebonnet. "We're moving so fast." She looked out the window and watched the sky change from bright blue to black.

"Bluebonnet! Come in! Are you there?" Bluebonnet heard a voice in the speakers of her earflaps.

"Normadillo!" Bluebonnet squealed in amazement. "Where are you?"

"I'm at Mission Control!" said Normadillo. "Oh, Bluebonnet! I've been so worried about you. Are you okay?"

"I'm fine!" Bluebonnet reassured her sister. "But how did you get into Mission Control?"

"I snuck in here. I just had to find out about you," said Normadillo anxiously. "I'm hiding behind a computer. The room is full of people at computer terminals, watching two big screens. One has a map of the world, and a line going across it to keep track of the shuttle's orbit. The other is like a television, so I'll be able to see pictures of you inside the shuttle."

"Ohhh," moaned Bluebonnet.

"What's the matter?" Normadillo asked in an alarmed voice.

"I can barely move," said Bluebonnet. "It's like an invisible force is pushing against me."

"It's three times the force of gravity on Earth," said Normadillo. "Remember? The movie we saw at the Space Center called it three g's."

Suddenly, the booster rockets cut off and the force was gone. The giant boosters fell into the ocean.

"Whew," said Bluebonnet in a relieved voice. "That feels much better."

"According to the information on my computer, you're fifty miles above the earth," said Normadillo. "The shuttle's engines will take you into an orbit two hundred miles above Earth. You will be traveling five miles a second, and it will take you ninety minutes to go around the earth once. You will watch sixteen sunrises and sixteen sunsets every twenty-four hours."

"Ahhh!" exclaimed Bluebonnet.

"What's the matter now?" asked a concerned Normadillo.

"The earth is so beautiful!" Bluebonnet replied. "I can see the blue oceans, the orange deserts, the mountain ranges, and the twinkling city lights! I wish you were here with me, Normadillo."

"Mission Control is an exciting place to be, too," said Normadillo. "I'll stay right here, Bluebonnet, and check in with you from time to time."

Bluebonnet giggled. "I read you loud and clear, Normadillo. Over and out."

The astronauts let Bluebonnet out of her straps. Together, they floated around and turned flips.

"How about some dried insects?" said an astronaut. "We brought several packages just for you."

"Not bad," thought Bluebonnet as she munched on her special treat.

Bluebonnet watched the astronauts' activities. They floated around the cabin, busily at work with cameras and calculators. Bluebonnet curled up in a ball and floated about the cabin until she finally went to sleep.

"Bluebonnet? Bluebonnet!" an astronaut's voice awakened her. "It's time for our space walk."

Bluebonnet blinked her eyes. She had been moved to the air lock below the flight deck. Two astronauts were dressed in space-walk suits, holding a special clear plastic space suit made especially for her. They attached it to her helmet. The space suit had a small pack containing an oxygen supply and temperature controls.

As the hatch closed, the astronauts attached thin wires to themselves and to Bluebonnet. They waited until the air was pumped out of the air lock. Then they opened the hatch and floated out into space!

"Wow!" squealed Bluebonnet. "The stars look so much closer."

"All right, Bluebonnet," said one of her astronaut friends. "Can you move around for us?"

Bluebonnet curled up and spun around. The astronauts took pictures of her many movements. In the middle of a somersault, she noticed the bright blues and greens of the earth below.

"How beautiful the earth is!" Bluebonnet said.

"Earth to Bluebonnet!" a voice called over her helmet speaker.

"Normadillo! I'm walking in space!" Bluebonnet exclaimed.

"I can see you here at Mission Control," Normadillo said.

"You can?" Bluebonnet looked at her astronaut friends, who were filming her space walk. "Well, hello, Normadillo!" she smiled and waved.

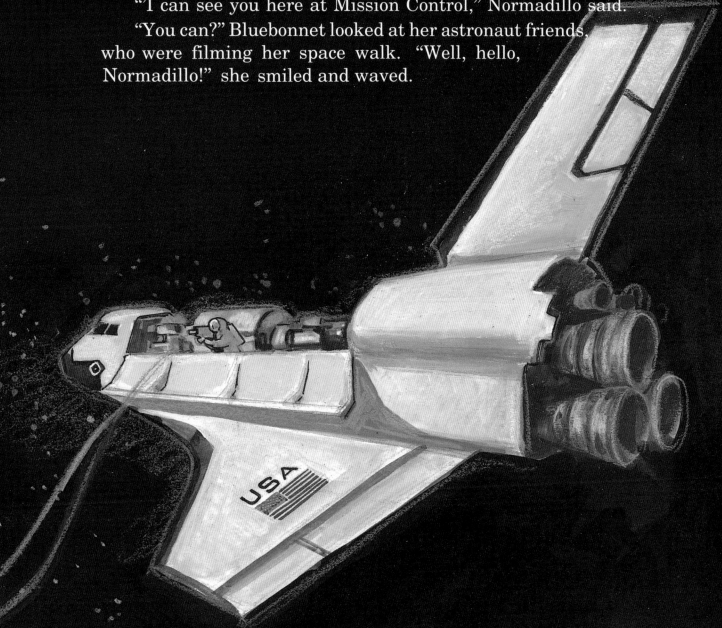

"You know, Bluebonnet, you're not such a silly dilly after all," said Normadillo. "You're the world's first astrodillo! I'm proud of you!"

"Good work, Bluebonnet," said her astronaut friends. They continued to film her movements. "Perhaps one day we will have space suits as flexible and protective as your shell."

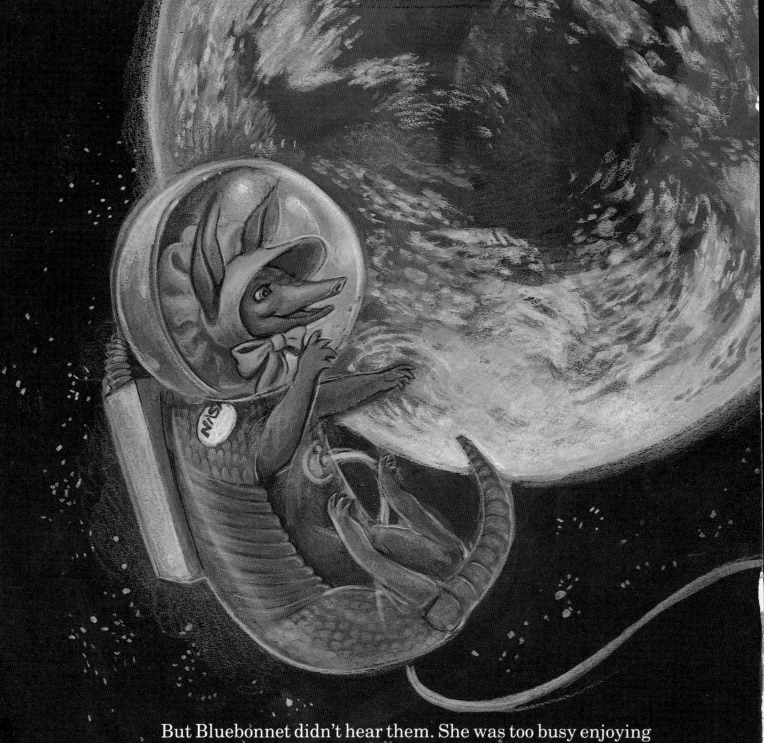

But Bluebonnet didn't hear them. She was too busy enjoying her space walk. As she moved about, she remembered her many dreams of becoming an astrodillo. They had finally come true.

"Bluebonnet? Bluebonnet!" the astronauts called to her. Bluebonnet finally turned around and moved back towards the shuttle.

"We'll soon be leaving to head back to Earth, but will you be ready to go with us on a mission to Mars?" they asked.

And Bluebonnet the astrodillo took another look at the stars and smiled. She would be ready, as always, for more adventures!